Hardcover ISBN 978-0-6459887-7-2

Paperback ISBN 978-0-6459887-0-3

eBook ISBN 978-0-6459887-1-0

Audiobook ISBN 978-0-6459887-6-5

Published by Jade Press

Daidállō

For my son, Lewis.

Because of you, this happened.

... At first a herald flash

Just chased the darkness, and the thunder spoke,

Breaking the strange tranquillity. But soon

Pale horror reigned, – the mighty tempest burst

In wrath appalling; – forth the lightning sprang

And death came with it, and the living writh'd

In that dread flame-sheet.

Dartmoor (1826)

N. T. Carrington

I put a spell on you, because you're mine.

Slotkin & Hawkins (1956)

1

The old man stared at me, his arms resting on the small square table between us. He had leant forward slightly– poised– as if waiting for me to give him a sign: some indication, some spark of recognition. It wasn't coming any time soon.

"The name," he said. He had repeated it, a little slower this time. "You've surely heard the name." It was a statement more than a question, but I was clearly being pressed to respond.

"I can't say I have," I admitted, an awkward almost embarrassed smile starting to grow on my face.

"*Volundr*," he said, repeating it again. His thick West Country accent played with the vowels and the consonants. On his tongue the word became 'VOH-l'nderrr'. In front of us sat two pints of beer, freshly pulled, inviting. They would have to wait a little longer.

"No. Not really. I don't think I *have* heard it before." I had nothing for him. Nothing except another empty smile.

"Oh, I'm sure you have," said the old man, smiling back at me. "In some form or another. Volundr is everywhere. Everywhere is Volundr."

After everything that had gone before, I was seeing him properly for the first time. He was still wearing his dirty green Barbour jacket. It was unzipped now and fell open past the sides of the chair. The right poacher's pocket was torn, revealing a square of less faded waxed cotton behind it. The wide, corduroy collar was drenched from the recent downpour and flopped heavily against the shoulders of the jacket. In the midst of it: a wild, grey beard spread out like an overgrown hedgerow, claiming territory usually reserved for the collar, and threatening to overrun the chequered shirt, jacket– all of it. On his head was an old woollen beanie: brown in places, green in others; its original colour lost to time. Like the jacket, the beanie was still wet. It was distracting me. I wanted to suggest that he take them both off; to dry them properly by the fire. On reflection, it crossed my mind that the jacket, beanie and man might actually be inseparable. The phrase weathered and worn could have been applied to all three in equal measure.

"Many names have been given to him though," he went on. "As many names as the stories that have been told."

"Ah, I see. So, I probably know him by a different name," I concluded.

"Maybe," he said, "Many names, many tales… Some are there to amaze, some to inspire… Some are bedtime stories, told to children to get them to sleep… Some to fill 'em with fear! In some he is the stout-hearted hero, battling adversity and tyranny. In others he is a cruel and cunning villain, hell-bent on vengeance and murder. You can take your pick, really."

The old man had promised me a story. Something to while away the time as we waited. But all this lead up, all this introduction… I hadn't expected this. It was a strange way to have started and I was struggling to get my head around it. Beside us the fire sputtered; the fresh wood added upon our arrival stirring it back from its slumber. The trails of smoke tickled at my nostrils, slowly pushing away the smell of wet clothes– soon it would disburse, be replaced by the flames that flicked already, stretching out from beneath the log: a promise of warmth, of a welcome dryness soon to come.

"To some he's a blacksmith," he said. "A bladesmith, even a goldsmith... To others he's a warrior, a wizard– Ha!– Even a god."

"Ah! Soooo this sounds like a... *Medieval story...?*" I said. Maybe we were getting somewhere...

"If you want." The old man seemed disinterested in my attempt to pin definition on what he was saying. "Some have Volundr crafting swords, it's true. Like *Caliburn*, the sword he made for Merlin. Others have him in much earlier times... Some as a kind of magical figure, making indestructible armour, creating life even... Volundr has been an architect of churches, the destroyer of kingdoms. He's in songs, poems, depictions on stone crosses, ancient caskets… He even appears in that book at Exeter Cathedral… You must've heard of him."

I took a sip of beer. I looked across at the old man once again. Pale blue eyes sparkled behind large gold-framed glasses. They were open wide, and a smile was breaking through the undergrowth of beard. Once again, he was waiting for a glimpse of realisation from me. Blacksmiths… Merlin… 'ancient caskets'. This *was* starting to sound familiar.

"Are we talking about *Wayland*?" I asked. "The Smith?" I had a vague recollection of this. Some story I had heard as a child. Somewhere I'd visited in Oxfordshire too… But it was distant, hazy for me… Were we talking mythology? Was that it? Was this the legend of Wayland the blacksmith?

"If you like," he said. "Volundr has been known by that name. That's the old English telling. But as I say: Volundr is everywhere. Everywhere is Volundr," the old man repeated. He seemed to take great pride in this statement.

Okay. This'll do, I thought. I could work with this. Anything to take my mind off work. I knew I was just putting off what needed to be done, but the old man and his story could be the distraction I needed. Besides, everything I should have been doing was back at the car.

"So, what version do we have here, then?" I asked, hoping that he was about to make a start now.

"You'll decide for yourself, I'm sure," said the old man, settling into his chair with a smug smile.

2

I had been driving too fast when it had happened. The Nissan Qashqai had slipped easily through the Devon countryside, heading North from Princetown. I had visited my boss at his house. It had taken longer than I'd expected. Now I was running late. Still much to do. Still a long way from where I needed to be. Soon, Sarah would start to worry, start to wonder where I was.

I knew the road well though. I had often used it as a shortcut back to the North of the county. Driving from Plymouth to Barnstaple, the main roads were by far the quickest option, but with

Nuth moving here, choosing Princetown, there was no avoiding the B3212, the Dartmoor road. Today in particular. Through Two Bridges, Moretonhampstead, then across to Whiddon Down... I'd travelled these roads many times before. The weather was good, visibility was clear, and the new car could take the corners well. She would've looked a fine sight too, slicing through the countryside in the late afternoon sun: stark white against the backdrop of the moor. Almost new. Only 500 miles on the clock. On the passenger seat was my jacket. I would probably need it later. On the backseat was my laptop. *So much still to do.* I didn't see the pony until it was almost too late.

It was standing sideways in the middle of the road, unmoving– just staring straight ahead. I swerved sharply to the right, to avoid hitting the animal. The tyres screeched as I braked. I was at a T junction and suddenly the car was skidding onto the intersecting road, then OFF the intersecting road and onto the grass verge next to it. Somehow, I had missed the pony, missed the Give Way sign… and sadly, missed the road too. The car had come to rest with its front bumper half-buried in the Devon hedgerow that lined the road.

My heart was still racing when I got out of the car. I opened the driver's door gingerly, so as not to hit it against any rocks hidden in the earthy bank. I stopped beside the car, looking across from the intersection to the road where only moments before, I had been happily travelling; the road where the pony had been.

Wild Dartmoor ponies were everywhere here. They owned these moors. Most locals knew better than to interfere with them. In the past I had seen many a tourist bitten or kicked, as they attempted to feed or pat one. This one was long gone now; snapped out of its daydream, or slumber or trance– or whatever the hell that was– by the sound of my squealing tyres, and the sight of me careering into a hedge. Not my finest hour. *What had it been playing at?* All that was at this T junction now was the road sign: to the right was 'M'hampstead'; to the left Postbridge, Princetown and back the way I'd come.

In the breast pocket of my shirt were my cigarettes. I pulled one out of its packet and lit it. *Just something to settle the nerves*, I thought. I straightened my tie, then moved around the car to inspect it. How there was no damage I didn't know. It wasn't even muddy from mounting the grass verge. As I looked down at the passenger side wheel arch, a drop of ice-cold rain hit the back of my neck and slid down my shirt collar. I straightened up and looked at the sky. Thick, dark clouds were building overhead, reminding me that this was Dartmoor: elevated, exposed, closer to the heavens and– here, on cue– the rain was coming.

"I need to get going," I said, to no one in particular, throwing down the cigarette as I reached the driver's side door again and slipping back into the car. The engine started easily, as the first real drops of rain hit the windscreen. I turned on the wipers, put the car into reverse, and it– shuddered wildly, refusing to move.

The rain was really coming down now, hammering against the roof of the car, pouring down the windscreen. In the distance was the first rumblings of thunder... This damned moor. It could be so generous one minute and so cruel the next. For some reason I was stuck, and I needed to work out why. I was stuck here; at the junction they called The Watching Place.

There were so many eerie places on Dartmoor, many attributed with strange and sinister tales. The Watching Place was no exception. The story goes that a local lord of the manor had once erected gallows on this spot, at the edge of his land. They were used to hang thieves and highwaymen. Legend has it that many were left to swing for days– long after their deaths– serving as a warning to others. Friends and family of the condemned were made to wait and watch over the corpses, before finally being permitted to cut them down. Hence the grim name given to this T junction. Dartmoor was full of strange folklore like this. Many of the stories were well-known. The tourists lapped them up like Devonshire cream teas.

In one corner of the intersection was Beetor Cross, perched high on the opposite bank; one of many ancient Dartmoor crosses, carved from granite and scattered throughout the landscape. This one was aptly nicknamed The Watcher: keeping a solitary vigil over the junction. To either side of the cross were old moss-covered oaks; remnants of a once great moorland forest... Five minutes earlier the sun would have been hitting these trees, flooding the scene with an emerald hue that would tempt any amateur photographer to capture that magnificent grey man in all his stoic glory: draped in his ivy garland and framed by ancient oaks. Now that miserable old rock loomed over me in silent judgement: in my mind the gnarled and twisted limbs of the trees seemed almost to be reaching for me– pointing, mocking, daring me to come closer. I was going to have to. I needed to know why the car wouldn't reverse, why I couldn't get back onto the road. I was going to have to get out there, into that rain again. I was staring at The Watcher through the passenger window, all of this running through my mind, when the face appeared at the glass.

"You've got a flat!"

"What!" I must've leapt back in my seat, visibly shocked by the sudden appearance of the silhouette at the side of the car. The man must have seen my surprise, as his hands raised to eye level, palms facing out, gesturing submissively.

"A flat tyre. You've got a flat. *Your side*," he said, pointing over the bonnet. I glanced across the front of the car. It was true. I could see it now, even through the rain. The driver's side of the car was definitely much lower, as if the right corner was sinking slowly into a Dartmoor bog.

"You need to get your spare!" The man was shouting over the sound of the rain.

"What?" I leant over the passenger side and opened the car door a little. "Get in," I said, throwing my jacket on to the back seat to make room for him. "You're soaked."

"No," he said. "We need to get this done. We need to get your spare out."

"I don't have one," I said.

"What's that? No spare?! Who doesn't 'ave a spare?"

"Me. I don't. Look— get in, buddy. You're drenched!" The man looked quite old from what I could see, which wasn't much. Young or old though, he probably shouldn't have been out in this weather. Rain was pouring over the lip of his beanie, running into his face.

"This looks like a *new* car!" he said, continuing to stand there, shouting through the gap in the passenger door, a surprised tone to his voice. "Why doesn't it have a spare tyre?!"

"It is. It was an option. I ticked NO."

"Who ticks NO?"

"I do. I needed the boot space– Look, mate–"

"I can help," he said quickly. "Get in mine," he continued, gesturing over his shoulder with a nod of his head. I cast a look in the rear-view mirror. There, across the intersection on the main Dartmoor road, a small blue van was parked, its hazard lights blinking warmly in the rain.

"I can't leave the car!"

"You can't stay *here*, in this. *This*," he said, gesturing vaguely, half towards the car, half towards the dark, grey sky overhead. "You can't be doing *this*. This is a fate worse than death, this is."

It was true I couldn't just stay here. I needed to get going. In the rear-view mirror I could see the inverted image of the signpost on the other road: right– or left now– was Moretonhampstead,

17

Okehampton; left– or right– was Princetown, Plymouth and back the way I'd come. I needed to go North, to get off this moor, eventually. Eventually get home. This man was gesturing South.

"There's a pub, not far down," he explained. "I'll take you to a phone." Of course! The Warren. I had passed it on the way up. It would be warm there…

"Okay," I said, beginning to get out of the car. There really was no choice to be made. Everything else was going to have to wait. I'd get to the phone, call a recovery vehicle. It would swing by, pick me up, and we'd be back here at the intersection in no time. We'd replace the tyre, and–

"A nail."

"Sorry?" I said. We were at the van now. I was brushing the wet hair from my face.

"Your flat tyre," the old man explained, talking across the roof of the van. "It looked like there was a nail there."

"Oh," I said, as I got into the passenger seat, slamming the door shut and closing off the elements. I must've driven over an old piece of timber as I slid onto the grass beside the road. Something hidden in the turf, perhaps. "Thanks for doing this."

"'Pleasure. Glad I could help," he said, smiling through his beard. "I'm Borkham. That's what everyone 'round here calls me," he explained. "Borkham."

"Thanks, Borkham. It– It got so dark…" We were off and moving now. Heading South, back the way I'd come.

"You'd thrown a shoe!"

"Huh?"

The old man smiled. "The flat tyre. You'd thrown a shoe."

"Ha! Yes– I suppose I had." I laughed at the old saying. Horseshoe. Tyre. Only in Devon… This was good though. I could sit this out in the pub. Maybe get some work don– And then I realised: I had left my phone, my laptop, EVERYTHING back at the car. In my hurry to get into the van, to get out of the elements, everything else had been forgotten. Work had been so hard of late. I was so tired, so stressed. There was so much still to do. But it was too late to ask him to go back. We were back on the main Dartmoor road again, speeding through the countryside, this time in the opposite direction. And leaving all of that behind.

Very soon we were on a straight stretch of road and passing by Bennett's Cross. I watched it slide by from the passenger window. Sitting back from the road in open moorland, this twisted granite form seemed to point to the blackened sky, reminding me of what this landscape could deliver. Sitting there, my hands resting across wet trousers, my cold shirt clinging to my arms, my shoulder blades… it was a reminder I most certainly did not need. But we were on the part of the road that led to the Inn now. *Not far*, I thought. *Warmth is not far away*. And then– suddenly– there it was.

Warren House Inn rose up from the moor to greet our approach. Washed a ghostly white, and with smoke forever rising from its chimneys, it offered itself as a beacon as we moved along the straight stretch of road from the Northeast.

The history of The Warren was well-known to everyone in this area. The original Inn had been built to serve the workers from the tin mines that had nestled in the nearby valleys. These days it played host to locals, tourists and hikers; anyone that enjoyed a pint of ale, a warm open fire, and the views of the moor from this lofty perch. All of the above appealed to me now, as we pulled over to park out front.

It was still raining hard; the wind shoving at us as we left the car to make our way to the Inn's porch. We leant forward against the weather, staggering towards the doorway. Above us, set back into an old, enclosed window, hung the green sign of the freehouse: three rabbits chasing each other in a circle.

Somewhere not far off, a single thunderclap rang out. Despite our safe harbour, the storm would have the final word.

Inside, the Inn was quiet except for the murmur of a few voices and the crackle of the open fire at one end. In here was indeed the warmth and refuge we had craved; the antidote to the weather we were shutting out, that we were leaving beyond its walls. The smell of wood smoke and the sweet scent of old beer blended to create the familiar welcome of a country Inn, heightening the scene before us and igniting the imagination. For despite its peacefulness, its calmness, the Inn was a symphony for the senses and such a contrast to its simple white exterior. Low ceilings with exposed oak beams drew the eye to corners and crannies where trinkets and treasures lay, waiting to be discovered: clay bottles, brasses and row upon row of china plates and other knick-knacks. Prints depicting local scenes pressed themselves against wood-panelled walls while an upright piano standing proudly by offered a testament to evenings of song and celebration: those that had been, and those yet to come. At the centre of it all, the modest bar; illuminated, prominent, crammed with bottles, tankards and wineglasses and beckoning the weary traveller to lean awhile, to linger and imbibe all they saw, all they heard, all they felt…

At the bar, we were met by the landlord and two young men who had clearly taken up this offer. I ordered us two ales. I asked if I could use the telephone, explaining what had happened further up the road. Of course I may. The people here were friendly, helpful, accommodating. It was in their make-up. I called the recovery service. We talked it through: *Swing by, pick me up, head back to the intersection at The Watching Place*. Pretty straight forward. It shouldn't be more than an hour or so away. Meanwhile we could settle in beside the fire. It would be a chance to dry off, warm up and perhaps order some food.

Before this nineteenth century building, the original Inn– the 'New House'– had been located on the opposite side of the highway, operating from as early as the late seventeen hundreds. Long before that, they say a Bronze Age settlement had been located close by– so many remnants of huts and longhouses scattered throughout the moor. Like their Cornish counterparts, the ancient mines here had supplied the much-sought tin to the early trade lines of Europe and beyond. There was just so much *history* in this place...

As we moved through the bar and towards a small table by the fire, I wondered how many carts and packhorses had passed through; how many feet had trodden this path... It wasn't hard to imagine this place frozen in time, cut off from the outside world. On particularly harsh winters this had been known to happen, for weeks on end.

The nights were drawing in now, but we were still a few months away from midwinter. And yet– that same sense of being frozen, removed from time and space, seemed to hang in this place. As we sat there at that table, in that moment… we could've been anywhere, anywhen.

I wondered if Sarah would like it here.

"You look like you need an escape."

"I'm sorry?" The old man's words pulled me back from my recollection.

"An escape. This story is about escape. Escaping a fate worse than death. Just like you, eh? Ha!" He stared at me; a bright smile splashed across his face. It was as if we were sharing a joke;

a double entendre, a secret quip between two old friends.

"I don't get it," I said. I was frustrated. I had thought the story was starting.

Borkham gestured vaguely towards the door of the Inn. "Back there," he said, the smile starting to fade now. "All of that. That junction."

"Ah yes– the weather. It got dark so quickly. And that RAIN!"

"Rain," he mumbled. The old man waved his right hand, absently, dismissively. His face was serious now.

"Anyway. Let's get into it," he said.

And so finally, the story began.

3

"Like his many names, Time has given Volundr many birthplaces. For the sake of our tale though, we'll put him in Scandinavia. A simple man born into village life… a couple of hard-working parents… He's surrounded by Finnish birch trees and– we'll set him up somewhere near craggy Baltic cliffs. That sort of thing."

So much for setting the scene, I thought. This was sounding thrown together. What had I expected from this dishevelled old local though? I hoped that Borkham's story-telling abilities would improve as he got underway. Otherwise, the next hour or so might really drag.

"Volundr had two older brothers," he went on. "Egil and Slagfinn. As young boys they'd roam the nearby area, explore the forest, hunt together... The boys loved each other's company; inseparable. They'd get lost for hours— sometimes days— learning to hunt and fish, crafting basic tools... contraptions. Nature was their classroom. They were fast learners. Each developed their own skills, own strengths. Egil took to archery and inventing, Slagfinn— hunting. Volundr— crafting. Although each could rival the other if he turned his mind to it. Years passed. Eventually fun had to give way to making a living. Their father sent each boy away to learn a trade. Volundr was send to the mountains in Iceland to learn smithing. Metalwork, stonework... He missed his older brothers but vowed to commit to his apprenticeship. In the mountains he grew from boy to man, from novice to craftsman. And when his apprenticeship finally ended, he returned to his homeland as he'd promised and was reunited with Egil and Slagfinn.

"They set themselves up in the forest close to their home village. They built a hunting lodge and a small smithy and workshop. Here they applied their skills: building, repairing and wrighting; trading in game and furs... and of course: blacksmithing. Time hadn't changed them much– not really. And the boys– now men– continued much as they'd done before. Except this time with coins in their pocket and beer in their bellies. Cheers." Borkham raised his glass and took a generous drink of ale.

"Cheers," I replied with a smile and did the same. Borkham seemed to be getting into his stride now. I was curious to see where this story would go. He continued.

"The young men would set out deep into the forest to hunt or fish. Sometimes they would go in pairs, sometimes solo… They were happiest though when the three were hunting together: it reminded them of their childhoods and their adventures as young lads. Nothing would please them more than to be in the wilderness– smelling it, tasting it; an arm around the shoulder of their kin…

"It was as the three brothers prepared for such a trip that it happened, the incident at the lake.

"Egil, Slagfinn and Volundr were gathering together their equipment for a two-day hunt when they heard a commotion overhead. It was the sound of large wings beating air, a rustling in the branches… something brushing against the foliage. Something, or some *things*, they thought,

31

as the noise continued for a number of seconds. It was like a flock passing by. The brothers looked at each other, as if informed by the sounds: *Whooper swans!* Four or five at least, judging by the noise. Fine meat, and feathers that would be useful for sale or trade. They reached for their bows and set off in the direction the sound had travelled.

"Soon the three were approaching the place where the forest broke at a lake. The brothers knew it well. It was close to their lodge and a prime spot for trout fishing. Today the sound of splashing was much louder though: the birds had landed on the water for certain. They were washing now maybe, or hunting for food themselves: little fish, frogs… Signalling to each other in silence, the three brothers agreed to separate: to spread out and approach the lake from different positions. If the birds were startled by their arrival– if they attempted to fly– the men would have three different angles to fire their arrows from. This would increase their chances of catching these large birds.

"Volundr stepped quietly through the thicket– the last of the forest before it gave way to the grassed bank of the lake. It was early morning: the wintry sun had risen to the treetops directly ahead, glinting on the lake and sending ripples of white light to splash against the treeline. He raised his arm to shield his eyes from the sun as he broke through... But something was not right. He thought he could hear voices, laughter... Volundr stepped forward, blinded, confused. His boot caught on something underfoot and he almost lost his balance. He looked down. There at his feet was a pile of clothes and swan-white feathers. Close by, either side of him, Egil and Slagfinn had similarly stepped from the forest. They were frozen now, stunned– unable to fully take in the scene before them. Egil dropped his bow.

"Alerted by the noise, the three bathing maidens covered themselves with their arms. They were equally surprised to see the three men. Nearby, a startled pheasant took to the air."

Borkham had stopped talking. He was looking down. Between his fingers was a short length of brown string. He had retrieved it from a pocket in his Barbour jacket and was winding it and unwinding it on the index finger of his left hand.

"What happened next?" I asked, nudging him to continue the story.

"They were married for nine years," he said. "Each brother had taken one of the women as a wife. They were Valkyries– warrior maidens, royal daughters. They had taken a pause from their service in battle to bathe in that lake. Some say the brothers stole their flying suits– their means of escape– entrapped them there. The truth though is far from that. Nine blessed years at the lodge by the lake. The three couples enjoyed the happiest times of their lives."

"So, why only nine years?" I asked.

"Duty, perhaps." he said. "As simple as that. It is true that *at first* the swan-maidens had found it hard to adapt to mortal life. But the love they felt for the three brothers was pure and true, and that alone would have been enough to see them remain. But 'Fate goes ever as Fate must' and Odin sends his slain choosers to every battle after all. Maybe somewhere a war was being waged, and they had heard its call. They would've had no wish to feel the fury of the Val-Father himself, fearing banishment from Valhalla. Or maybe as Odin's heralds of death, they worried that their presence there may eventually mark their

35

beloveds and bring about their demise… Either way, the three men returned from hunting one day to find their wives had gone."

I looked across to Borkham. I'd wanted to hear more about the brothers and their wives. Their years together, their lives together. I imagined the warrior maidens sparring with the men, honing their battle skills— in every way their equals. I could see them becoming expert hunters like their husbands, quiet moments at the cottage… Perhaps the men learnt new skills themselves: horse-handling, manipulating beasts and birds… But Borkham was staring into his tankard, and I knew that *this* wasn't the tale I would hear today. Like the ale though, the story was still a long way from finished. And so I said:

"Go on." And so he did.

"Anguished and heartsick, the brothers were determined to find their brides. It was decided:

Egil would search East, Slagfinn to the South. Someone needed to stay behind, and so Volundr remained at the lodge to await everyone's return.

"Weeks passed. Then months. Volundr was heartbroken. He missed his wife. He missed the companionship of his older brothers. He found solace in the only thing he knew: smithing. Again, Volundr threw himself into his craft. He continued to shoe horses, wheel carts, cooper... he even fashioned simple rings. The lonely man enjoyed the company that custom brought. Often, he refused to take money from the local villagers for the work he had done. He claimed their smiles and thankyous were payment enough. He lived at the lodge. He worked. He hunted. He waited.

"Already a highly skilled smith, Volundr began to branch out: swordsmithing, making armour, working gems... He made himself a sword: he broke it down again, time after time, reforging it, adjusting it… perfecting it … He added jewels… Finally, he had crafted the legendary blade, *Mimmung…*

"Volundr began to work more and more with precious metals, his favourite task being to craft rings. When the swan-maidens had left the lodge, they had left behind the three rings that Volundr had made for them. The two brothers had taken their wives' rings with them when they had set off on their searches, tying them to string around their necks. Staying behind, Volundr placed his wife's ring on the branch of a willow tree outside the lodge. He set his mind to making copies of that ring, in honour of his wife– one for every day that passed until she returned. Each day he would craft a new ring and tie the duplicate to the same tree. Soon the willow tree was laden with seven hundred rings.

"Over that time, Volundr's work became more elaborate: more ornate, more delicate... and more sought-after. His reputation spread wider than his local area. People came from all over Scandinavia and Northen Europe to seek out his skills. It was said that his armour and weapons could give an army an advantage in battle – 'the best of all war-shrouds'. His jewellery and gemwork was fit for a queen, they said. Soon his work was being commissioned, coveted... and of course, envied."

Borkham paused for a moment, leaning forward in his chair, his arms resting once again upon the table. "Some say it was the metallurgy they envied the most. The knowledge, the secret methods of production, the power the metals could hold. In those days, the ability to create such fine work... Some saw it as a magic of its own. Such were the reputations that these blacksmiths held. Some would see them as more powerful than any druid, any witch. They would claim that the swords these smiths crafted contained spirits; souls of their own that would do the bidding of whoever owned them, whoever wielded them. That other crafted items could become powerful talismans: instruments of the dark arts that could ward, could protect. Could summon even. The metals, the magic... for some it was all intertwined, all one and the same... and for them, this was what they desired above all else.

"But smithing... it was so closely guarded a skill! These metallurgists, they would not have given away the secrets of their trade, be they magic or otherwise. This only made them more valuable allies, more prized assets. And a highly skilled blacksmith such as Volundr, at the peak of his profession… his services would have been in very, very high demand.

"The Swedish King Nithad was a greedy man: greedy and jealous. He believed that Volundr's weaponry and jewellery should not be allowed to leave Scandinavia. More so, it should be the sole possession of his palace and his family. One winter's day Nithad and his Royal Guard came to visit Volundr's lodge. He bestowed compliments and gifts on the blacksmith. He was invited to leave the solitude of the forest and to travel with the king to the palace. Nithad spoke of wealth and prestige. He offered Volundr a seat at the royal table… He *must* become the kingdom's royal smith.

"Volundr declined. He stated that everything he could ever need was here in the forest; that he enjoyed serving the local villages and that he was duty-bound to remain at the lodge. Nithad was angered by this but remained outwardly calm. He smiled. He complimented Volundr on the fantastic tree of rings at the front of the lodge. He offered him a flagon of wine: *no hard feelings*. Volundr declined to drink. Nithad insisted he keep the wine. Perhaps there would be cause for them to drink together another time. Volundr watched as the king and his guards rode away from the lodge and back through the forest.

"The next day Volundr set off to hunt, as usual. On his return to the lodge, he was immediately struck by the sense that something was different– something was out of place. He knew every corner and every inch of the lodge and its surrounds, and something was wron– A RING! There was a ring missing from the willow tree! Volundr was overwhelmed with elation– his wife! She had returned! He rushed to the lodge, throwing open the door. There was no one inside:

the lodge was silent except for the occasional spit from the fireplace. But she was back, he was certain! Perhaps all three wives had returned, and they were now in the forest, looking for Volundr and his brothers! He hurried to tidy the lodge and to prepare it for their arrival! Nithad's flagon of wine sat on the great oak table. Volundr poured some into a wooden goblet. Just one glass to celebrate the impending return of his love...

"When Volundr awoke, he was no longer in the lodge. Cold, hard stone pressed against his face, and a chilled air blew all about him. He was face-down on a cobbled floor. His attempt to stand was in vain; partly from an intense weakness of his limbs, but more from the fact that his feet were bound and his arms were tied behind him. As he lay there, unable to right himself, he heard footsteps approaching, and soon his eyes were faced with two sets of boots.

Daidállō

He felt rough hands upon him and in a moment he was standing, staring at the insignia of the Swedish royal guard."

4

"Nithad," I concluded. I was staring straight at Borkham, absorbed by the story.

"Nithad," he agreed. "The wine had been drugged, and the soldiers waiting for their chance to grab him."

"So he's at the palace," I surmised.

"Yes. Miles from where he needed to be!" Borkham continued the story:

"The royal guards dragged Volundr through the palace and into a large open hall. Here Nithad was waiting for him, his queen Sinmara with him, more guards either side of the royal pair. The hall was immense: tall stone pillars, tapestries, oak dining tables... But Volundr had no interest in taking in the view; he did not care for castles or finery. He had been taken against his will. He needed to return to the forest immediately! He stated this to Nithad, his voice echoing off the stone in the vast space of the hall.

"Nithad chuckled. Perhaps he would be allowed to return to the forest, he said. Perhaps... in time. For now, Volundr was to remain here, to craft fine jewellery for the queen and his daughter, Bothvild and to forge powerful weapons, such as this: Nithad reached behind a large oak chair to reveal the sword, *Mimmung,* snatched from the lodge on the night that Volundr was taken.

"Volundr attempted to explain again that he was needed back at the lodge. Besides, surely the king had his own royal smith already. In response to this, Nithad simply bellowed through the hall to the guards outside. They entered, pushing a man ahead of them. He wore a suit of armour and a helmet. He was a short man, and the suit was too large for him. It clattered around him as he staggered into the hall. Nithad knocked the helmet from the man's head with the sword. He introduced the man as Amilias, the royal smith. He was the greatest maker of armour in all of the kingdom, said Nithad. This, he said, prodding at the suit with the sword, was the finest work that Amilias had mustered. Swinging the sword, Nithad struck the armour across the chest, cleaving it in two and killing the man in an instant. An opportunity had opened up, said Nithad, for a new royal smith.

"Volundr could see that there would be no arguing with Nithad: to continue to do so could bring him a similar fate. He agreed to work solely for the king. He promised to deliver him the finest weapons and jewellery. He asked that in exchange, Nithad allow him to return to his lodge to complete his work there. Nithad shook his head. The smith was to work close by, within the realms of the kingdom, where he could be watched over. However, he could work for his freedom. After a period of time Nithad would reconsider Volundr's offer. If he was satisfied with the work that had been done, perhaps then he could be allowed to return to his forest to continue there. Work hard for me, and we will talk again when the mid-summer festival arrives, Nithad said. Do not think of trying to leave in the meantime. Sweden owned a vast army that was highly skilled at searching for people, hunting a man down... and Nithad was not known for his forgiving nature. Volundr was accompanied to the edge of the town and placed on a boat. The boat carried him; winding down a river to an island on a great lake: where Amilias had lived and worked. Here he found a small cottage and an established smithy. And so began his work as Nithad's reluctant royal smith.

"Volundr longed to be home. His wife would be there now surely– worrying, wondering where he was. But on he worked. In his mind was the freedom he had been promised: the motivation to forge the best weaponry he had ever made, the finest jewellery, the most exquisite silverware… Once a week the king's guards would arrive to carry away the fruit of his toils. Soon he was receiving other visitors: the two young princes.

"The king's twin sons would arrive with a section of the royal guard that had been sworn to secrecy on pain of death. These spiteful boys would throw rocks at Volundr, insult him and threaten to set their guards on him if he did not make for them crude weapons to play with and trinkets to hoard. At first Volundr ignored the children, refusing to entertain their demands. After the third flogging from the royal guards, he began to comply.

"Spring came, and so did a visit from the king. Escorted by heralds and soldiers, Nithad arrived with Sinmara, the two young princes and his daughter, Bothvild. Volundr's sword *Mimmung* was strapped to his belt. Nithad had come to inspect Volundr's work and to take away more jewellery and precious gems. He told Volundr that he had also come with a specific task for the smith: his daughter's ring had become damaged, and he needed Volundr to repair it for her as a matter of urgency. Volundr agreed and asked to see the ring.

"Bothvild removed the glove from her hand and extended her arm towards the smith. There was no visible damage, but he recognised the ring immediately. It was the missing ring from the willow— his wife's ring— stolen! Volundr recoiled, as if from an approaching snake. He fell to the ground. Bothvild retracted her arm, laughing at the smith who for the first time was understanding the significance of the sight of this ring. Yes, said Nithad. It was his wife's ring. Did he think she had returned and discovered it? Oh! He did— he thought she was waiting back at the forest for him?

"Nithad began to laugh and was quickly joined by the queen and their daughter. The two young boys, ignorant to what was taking place around them, likewise began to laugh. It was as if Nithad had brought the entire royal family here just to mock the blacksmith and his misfortune. Did he see it now— Nithad asked— his fate? Your wife left you years ago, fool. Why would she return to this pathetic creature, he asked, pointing *Mimmung* at the fallen smith.

"Nithad had taken everything from him: his home, his sword, even the hope that he might one day see his wife again. Volundr was furious. He leapt to his feet; anger twisted across his face. He lunged towards the king and was immediately grappled by guards and wrestled to the ground once more.

"The royal family had been shocked by the attempted attack. Sinmara was visibly shaken, her face whitened by fear and disgust. She pointed at Volundr, proclaiming the blacksmith to be barely human, more wild beast than man. He needed to be kept here, she declared– in captivity on this island, for the safety of her family and the Kingdom. Pointing *Mimmung* at him again, Nithad angrily agreed: the smith had shown his true colours and must be prevented from striking out ever again. He took the sword, and with a single slash of the blade, cut through the hamstrings of Volundr's right leg. On the ground, the maimed Volundr screamed in agony. He was dragged back to his cottage by the king's guards and thrown onto its doorstep.

"Nithad turned now to his children, not to berate them for their treatment of Volundr but to issue them a warning: an animal was at its most dangerous when wounded. He forbade his three children from visiting the island again. Volundr should be left alone, to see out his days as the king's blacksmith. There should be no respite for him, no return to his beloved homeland."

The old man was interrupted as the Inn's landlord brushed past us to stoke the fire. I was suddenly dragged back from Wayland's captivity to the Inn on Dartmoor. Borkham's voice had been almost enchanting to me; drawing me in with its rustic tones, and its... No– that wasn't it. It was the opposite of that. Listening to Borkham, to his way of speaking: this story of a different world, from a different time… It was like a spell was lifting from me; like I was seeing things more clearly. It was like everything else was unimportant, unreal. Only this moment. This … simple story– this… innocent outlook. I stared at the fire, watching as two newly added hardwood logs popped and spat, the air in them expanding as the logs heated up and caught fire. New sparks shot out, and in no time, the fire was burning bright again.

The story goes that the fire in the hearth at Warren House Inn had never gone out; that the heat we felt from it today had begun in this hearth almost one hundred and eighty years ago. In fact, it was rumoured that smouldering embers had been carried from the old peat fire at the original

Inn across the road to light the first fire at the new Inn. It was a small hearth really: set within a large stone place and framed with thick oak, stained walnut in colour. On this hung half a dozen or so horse brasses; popular ornaments in these parts. A shelf had been attached to the original oak mantle, and on this were a number of blackboards, advertising the Inn's menu. It was from here that we had ordered food. To the left of the hearth, in a slight alcove, were black wrought iron fireplace tools: a poker and tongs. Next to these, leaning against the stone of the fireplace, was a large bellows. Into these the words WARREN HOUSE INN had been scorched. With the presence of these tools and bellows it was not hard to imagine a blacksmith's forge.

Borkham– so at home in a place like this! I could imagine him at the back door of the Inn, selling game that he had poached from a local farm, or blowing in from a full day of milking or shearing. Holding court with the patrons, spinning yarns... But his choice of story? Wayland...? It was so strange to be thinking about him here.

There was no real connection between the smith and this county, let alone the moor itself. Dartmoor stories were not about heroic blacksmiths or evil kings. This place spoke of witchcraft and devilry. Here were tales of misty moorlands, where demon dogs prowled, and unsuspecting victims were easily enchanted– led astray by pixies or evil spirits. It would make more sense to hear something about a local myth. Perhaps the mysterious and malevolent 'Hairy Hands' that appear on this very stretch of road: gnarled fingers that grab the steering wheel of cars or the handlebars of bicycles and motorbikes, dragging the vehicle from the road as it lurches into a stone wall or a ditch... Cutty Dyer– the throat-slitting sprite that terrorises children and drunks, throwing their lifeless bodies into the river Dart... Or the ghost of Childe the Hunter– the wealthy landowner who lost his way on the moor during a blizzard, taking shelter inside his disembowelled horse. Strange and unsettling events are said to befall anyone who spends a night on the land around Fox Tor Mires, a granite cross there, marking the spot where Childe's body is said to have been found... I could imagine a *Hammer Horror*-type story: Borkham telling a macabre tale of phantom horsemen, riding a skeletal steed– Tom Pearce's grey mare from Widecombe perhaps... Uncle Tom Cobley. How everyone seemed to love that old song... Maybe a story about a hitch-hiker he'd encountered... Something back at The Watching Place even. Something with a twist in its tale... I couldn't see a connection to this age-old story at all… But the fire was warm, the two servings of the Inn's famous rabbit pie had not yet arrived… and the old man had been kind: he'd driven me here, kept me company while I waited. There was no harm in humouring him, letting him tell his version of the blacksmith's story.

"Do you think there's any truth to it?" asked the old man. It was as if he had been reading my mind.

"To Wayland…?"

"Not *Vǫlundr*," he said, a little irritated. "The bloody fire. Do you reckon it's just for the tourists? They'll be telling us next that some Stone Age man first lit it." It was odd to hear Borkham become cynical about folklore, given our topic of conversation. I wasn't convinced he meant it. At that moment, he was reaching for the empty tankards on our table. "We're out of beer," he said gruffly. He looked awkward and in discomfort as he pulled himself to his feet. He seemed to be carrying an arthritic limp, agitated perhaps by the wooden chairs we were using. The bar was only a short distance away and the old man used his forearm to steady himself there as he waited for service.

"Let ME get these," I said, starting to stand.

"Nope– It's my round. Besides, here comes the grub," he said, gesturing with his head towards the other side of the bar. Heading back our way was the landlord, two plates in his hands. And soon, with fresh ales and a couple of servings of game, Borkham was continuing on.

5

"It started with the swans," he said.

"Volundr knew that Nithad had him beat. The vague notion of working 'til he was free had been exposed for the lie it was. Nithad's only intention had been to keep Volundr captive, forging weapons for his army and taking his finest crafts for his own. Also, he was a cripple now. It was no longer just 'where would he go?' But 'how?' So, he continued to slave away– for that was what he was now: Nithad's twisted and broken slave. Resigned to his fate, Volundr would work and sleep. He hunted, he ate, he lived. That was the sum of his life now. All the while Nithad continued to reap the rewards of Volundr's labour; his kingdom becoming the strongest and richest in all of Scandinavia.

"He was hunting one day when he first saw the swans. He had been tracking a bear through the woods, bow in hand, when he heard splashing coming from the nearby lake. He thought that the bear had spied a fish perhaps, and there would be an opportunity to take a shot at it while it was distracted. Volundr slowed his pace so as to quieten his steps, drew his bow, and there were–

"White-wings, darting past to land on the water– he was home! He saw himself with his brothers, Egil and Slagfinn: they were breaking through the tree line near their home. The lake had become their lake. Ahead of them came the sound of female voices, sweet laughter and splashing. He could smell leather and taste honey wine. At his feet was a pile of clothes and swan-white feathers. The

sun was glinting on the lake, sending ripples of white light across his face. He shielded his eyes to see—

"Swans. Just swans.

"There were five in total now, gliding gracefully on the water. They were grand, dignified, stately— every word you'd expect someone to use to describe those beautiful white birds. Everyone except Volundr. For he realised now that the sight of the swans had sent him into a wild reverie, an empty trick of the mind from which he now emerged. Volundr fell to his knees at the edge of the lake and wept. He wept for his brothers. He wept for his home. He wept for his wife and the life that he now knew was forever gone.

"One of the swans took flight, quickly followed by the others. Their webbed feet pressed on to the surface of the lake to gain traction. Their great wings slapped at the water as they slowly gathered speed; their long necks stretched out in front, as straight as an arrow. To see something this large and powerful take to the air would have been quite a sight. The lake was empty again now, except for a single *blop* of a trout catching a river fly, and in the distance a bird sang, calling to its mate. All of this passed by Volundr unnoticed, as he knelt at the lakeside, looking small now against the vastness of the wild.

"As much as it had hurt his heart to see the swans that day, in the days that followed, Volundr came to understand how those graceful birds offered him a connection to his past and the memory of happier times. As quickly as they'd arrived, the swans had gone. He hoped to see them again. He did not have to wait long.

"Around a week later the swans returned. The killing of them started quite by accident.

"The first swan landed on the bank of a river, near where Volundr was boar-hunting. Absent-mindedly, he drew his bow, as if to practice his aim. He made the noise of the arrow slicing through the air and hitting its target. And then– in a moment– he realised his grip on the bowstring had loosened. The arrow had flown. The bird was dead. Volundr panicked. The beak– an orange beak! This was not just a wild bird, not just a whooper swan. These were royal swans, *Nithad's swans*. Killing them was a crime, accident or no accident! He gathered up the dead bird, forced it into a sack, weighed it down with a rock and sunk it to the bottom of the lake.

"The second swan was different, and far from accidental. Something just came over him. It had landed in the clearing near the cottage. It was just... *there*. There was even plenty of time to retrieve the bow. The meat was useful, and it tasted all the sweeter for its source. The third and fourth... ah, it was almost a sport now. It turned out that killing the swans was easy. After a lifetime of hunting– well... plucking, beheading and gutting these large white creatures– it was... *routine* for Volundr. Killing was a means of survival, a necessity, and besides– it wasn't just swan meat that Volundr was getting a taste for. It was also a taste of freedom. These swans were symbols of Nithad's power and slaughtering them brought a strange sense of satisfaction to him. For the first time in a long while he found himself imagining freedom. As if eating the meat was giving him the power to take flight: to soar, to be liberated from this island prison, from the tyranny of the king, the torment of his sons, and the scorn of his wife and daughter. To be, as the saying goes–"

"*As free as a bird?*" I asked.

"Exactly. And it was in that moment that his plan began to form. It was the feathers, you see. The first day that the swans had landed on his lake– the day they had reminded him of the Valkyries, of his wife– they had also reminded him of the magical feather cloaks that the maidens had worn, giving them the ability to fly. Volundr remembered his childhood too, and the time spent with his two brothers. He remembered Egil in particular, not just as a keen archer, but as an inventor. He drew on the skills he had learnt from him. Using sewn pelts, fine soft metals and the large white feathers from the dead swans, Volundr crafted himself a flying contraption. He named it *Flygil*, in honour of his brother. Whenever opportunity allowed, and in secret– often under the shroud of darkness– Volundr would practice the art of taking flight in his invention, perfecting it as only a true craftsman might. But he did not fly away; not then. Fleeing the island was not the only thing on Volundr's mind. There was more to his plot than this, and there would be more to his craft too."

Borkham paused and stared intently into my face, holding my gaze earnestly. With a face as hard as a granite cross, he said:

"Prepare yourself, my friend. For the darkness is about to come." But I was way ahead of Borkham. I was remembering Wayland's story now.

"Killing the swans had been easy. Killing the two young Princes would be different. *That* would take time and patience. But time was the one thing Volundr had in abundance. And, as they say, 'all things come to those who wait'."

6

"The king's sons had been regular visitors to Volundr's island, and he knew that it was just a matter of time before they returned; coming to taunt him, steal from him, or to just enjoy watching him take another flogging. It was the daughter that returned first though.

"Volundr despised Bothvild. Not for the way that she flaunted his wife's ring in front of him at every opportunity. He despised her for her vanity and conceit. She was a plain girl, nothing much to look at, ugly in fact– both inside and out. Week after week she would visit Volundr on his island, her entourage of handmaids, attendants and guards in tow. How her maids fawned over her, primping and preening, complimenting her on her looks and grace. It disgusted him how she swelled from it; how it fed her ego and perpetuated the contemptuous manner in which she treated people, including the handmaids. Truth was, if she hadn't been Nithad's daughter, life would've kicked this shrew to a muckheap years back. But... there she was, *every week*: sniffing around Volundr's smithy, looking for what she could take.

"Visiting Volundr was still forbidden for all three of Nithad's children. Bothvild saw her trips to the island as a guilty pleasure– one she deserved– and as such she always expected some form of pay-off, whether it be by tormenting the smith with the sight of his wife's ring, dancing lasciviously around him as he tried to work, or slipping trinkets and gems into her garments, as Volundr pretended not to notice.

"As the weeks passed, Bothvild grew bored of these games and relaxed a little around Volundr. She could see that he was no threat to her, this bent up, hobbling old blacksmith. So, she would settle in and simply watch him work. She would engage him in casual conversation. Over time she brought less and less attendants and guards with her until finally Volundr was being visited by just Bothvild and her Lady's maid. It was on one such visit that Volundr told Bothvild that, *with her permission*, he should like to replace the old ring that she wore with a new one, much fancier and befitting a princess. Of course, Bothvild agreed on the spot. She gave up the old, dull ring that her father had gifted her on the promise of something much grander... And so began the next stage of Volundr's crafty scheme.

"Bothvild's visits continued. In fact, they intensified, until she was arriving at the smithy every other day. She would sit at Volundr's feet while he meticulously crafted the new ring. It would take some time, he said. But it would be the finest she had ever seen: so much detail, adorned with so many fine jewels. It would be ready in time for the mid-summer festival. She would turn heads there for sure, he promised. Volundr knew what words Bothvild needed to hear. And for Bothvild… she was warming to him, this generous craftsman. They began to share stories, to confide in each other. Volundr told Bothvild about his simple childhood and the fun he'd had in the Finnish forests. Bothvild spoke of her jealousy towards her two younger brothers, and of how she longed to be queen one day. Occasionally she would glance up at the blacksmith, this gentle, older man that listened to her and gave her advice– something her father had never done. They would exchange looks. He would smile kindly down at her. She felt something stirring in her heart: a fondness for this man that was slowly growing to become something more.

"Volundr's heart remained as stony as ever.

"Bothvild began to visit Volundr alone. There was something new about the way she spoke to him, the way she looked at him. It was softer, more familiar. It was easy for Volundr to mimic that look, that way of speaking: to show her the mirror she needed to see; to reflect that softness. Bothvild continued to visit every second day, staying later and later, sometimes into the evening. She would slip away as night fell. Once she was gone, Volundr would return to *Flygil*, and to perfecting his aerial skills. Eventually though, this would no longer be possible.

"Soon Bothvild was sharing with Volundr the feelings she had for him. And yes, he felt the same way, he said. He would break from his crafting to walk with her, leaving behind his birchwood crutch; instead Bothvild would offer his maimed body the support it needed. Hand in hand they would go: through the woodlands or beside the lake, pausing occasionally so that Bothvild could kiss his cheek. They would share meals at the cottage and in the evenings, they would nestle together and drink wine beside the open fire. Bothvild longed to take the feelings they shared for each other further. She knew she loved him, she said. And while Volundr felt the same, he declined her advances. He was adamant that they should wait. Volundr hinted at marriage: perhaps they should wait until then. The mid-summer festival was coming. He would speak to her father there. She agreed: she would not give herself to him; they would wait. He would ask Nithad for her hand on the evening of the mid-summer banquet. She would send a boat so that he could leave the island to attend.

"And so, the pattern formed: every second night Bothvild would fall into a deep slumber beside the fire. Every second morning she would wake at dawn in Volundr's bed, to find him sleeping on the ground next to the bed, wrapped in furs and a rug. Each time she would apologise. She would be embarrassed again; a little ashamed. She really had no head for wine, it seemed, and she would thank him for giving up his soft bed. Volundr would be understanding; tell her it was nothing, that she was more than welcome. Each time he would state that he enjoyed having her there and longed for the day when they could be together forever. They would share a hasty breakfast and she would scurry away, back to the mainland. Each time she would return the following day. The next day the same things would happen, all over again…

"The drug in Bothvild's wine was working well."

7

"The two young princes were six or seven years younger than their sister, but no less greedy and no less mean-spirited, as they had shown in their earlier visits. Like Bothvild, they had continued to visit Volundr's island, against their father's wishes, sneaking from the mainland with their royal guards.

"After the maiming of Volundr, the frequency of the boys' visits increased, as did their taunts: mocking his injuries, calling him names, throwing more rocks. It took all his will not to snap their tiny necks there and then. Instead, Volundr turned it into a game. Every time the boys threw a rock at him, he would thank them, claiming that he was so skilled a craftsman that he could turn this rock into a jewel. Every time the boys called him *cripple* or *freak* or *monster*, Volundr would agree, and claim to be the richest one in the entire kingdom.

"Eventually their curiosity got the better of them. The boys began to engage in conversation instead of abuse. They hung around Volundr, watching him work. Occasionally Volundr would drop hints about his hidden fortune, feeding their inquisitiveness. Oh yes, he would show them one day. Yes, yes, they would see. Soon... Soon... Every once in a while, the boys would leave with a trinket each; something to satiate them yet keep them hungry for more. It was like training wild dogs.

"Finally, the boys grew impatient. *They must see the treasure!* Volundr agreed and apologised for having kept them waiting for so long. He was concerned though, because he wasn't convinced the boys could keep the location of the fortune a secret. If their father found out about it, it would be taken from him, and Volundr would no longer be able to share it with them. The boys agreed to keep it quiet: the less people that knew about this the better. They would return in two nights, after dark, without their armed guard. They would sneak back to the island aboard a small boat. Volundr would show them everything. Volundr agreed. He promised them a sight they had never seen before. He promised them that they would never see anything like it again in their lives.

"Two nights later, the boys returned. It was dark when they knocked at the door of the blacksmith's cottage, their faces charged with a mixture of thrill, elation and impatience. Volundr opened the door and beckoned them into the cottage.

"In the centre of the room sat a large oak chest. It was a standard chest: unfooted, domed; perfect for travelling, if you were so inclined. It was rectangular, each side made from a single plank of oak. The pieces had been nailed together, then strengthened by thick iron bands. The bands themselves were both functional and decorative, forming a herring-bone pattern at the edges of the chest. Small wrought iron rings were positioned along the sides of the chest, adding more decorative elements. The front of the chest depicted a hunting scene, worked around a large lock plate at the centre of the panel: in the left of the picture stood a large, bearded man, poised with a bow and arrow, aimed at a doe near the centre. The doe was standing, head down as if grazing. On the ground under its belly a single adder writhed. At the man's feet two hunting dogs were sitting, poised as if waiting for their master's next command. An eagle flew at the far right of the picture, wings spread wide, soaring towards the iron bands at the edge of the chest.

"The boys could wait no longer and rushed over to the great oak chest. They knelt in front of it, hands on the lid. They tried to open the lid to look inside, but it was simply too heavy for their soft and weak little hands to lift. Volundr chuckled at their attempts. Patience, boys— patience. He walked over and rested his large hands on the edge of the closed lid; hands weathered from years of hard labour at the furnace and anvil. He paused for a moment, taking in the faces of the young boys as they looked up at him, almost quivering with excitement, anticipation, greed. Here, boys– look inside…

"Volundr imagined that the last thought that passed through the boys' meagre minds would have been one of confusion. They certainly wouldn't have understood why there was no fortune to be found in the great oak chest; why it was empty save for two simple woven baskets. They certainly wouldn't have seen the lip of the chest glinting in the firelight or have grasped how many hours it had taken Volundr to sharpen the fine blade that he had attached there– although they may have recalled watching him while he did so. Nor would they have heard the short grunt he made as he slammed the heavy lid shut with all his might: the baskets catching their prizes and the limp, headless bodies of the princes slipping forward against the oak.

"Volundr disposed of the boys' remains in the lake– well… most of it at least. He weighed it down in sacks of rocks. He sunk the small boat that had carried them from the mainland. Then he got to work. The festival and the mid-summer banquet were the following day, and he knew that if he was to succeed in his plan, he would have to work all night. There was so much still to do."

8

"The next day Volundr arrived on the mainland in the late afternoon, courtesy of the boat that Bothvild had sent. It carried him from his island on the great lake, up the meandering river to the outskirts of town.

"As he made his way through the town and towards the castle, he noted that it was very subdued there, considering today was the first day of the mid-summer festival. There were banners and flags a-plenty, carts of food and baskets of freshly cut flowers; quite a colourful sight, I'm sure. But it was like something had drained all the enthusiasm out of the day. The people he passed in the town did not share the bright smile that Volundr wore. Nor did they wave back at him, as he dragged himself through the cobble streets, a large bag over one shoulder. Soon, he was approaching the footbridge that led to the castle and over one of its narrow moats. No one challenged him as he entered; the castle's entrances were as bereft of soldiers as the nearby streets had been.

"King Nithad was standing in the great hall with his queen, Sinmara, much as he had the last time Volundr had been there. This time they wore ceremonial dress; Nithad with *Mimmung* on his belt. He was trying in vain to comfort the queen. She wailed and hammered her hands against the long dining table that she was slumped against; the sound echoing through the vast stone chamber. Nithad pulled at her dress sleeves, attempting to help her up, to reason with her. He was shocked to see Volundr as he limped into the great hall. Volundr raised a hand, gesturing that he meant no harm to the couple. This did not prevent Nithad from calling out for his royal guards. No soldiers came. It was the daughter that arrived next.

"Bothvild explained to the king that it was she who had invited Volundr to the castle; that he should be treated as her guest. She looked over to Volundr, barely able to contain herself at the sight of her beloved. He looked different to her though. His clothes were dirtier, his hair messier, his eyes wider than usual. He held her gaze for a moment and there, Bothvild saw the secret love they shared. It was in the smaller spaces of his face: in the corners of his mouth, the shape of his lip, the light in his eyes. Everything else was meaningless, a distraction.

"Nithad ignored Bothvild's words and stepped forward, one hand on the hilt of the sword. He meant to remove her lover from the hall! Bothvild would not allow this. She stepped between the two men, as if to defend Volundr. She claimed she had witnessed with her own eyes the changed man he had become in recent months. This angered the king, who reminded Bothvild that she had been forbidden from visiting the island. He would address this with her later. For now, there were more pressing matters to attend to, as well she knew. While he was suspicious of Volundr, consoling the queen was his primary concern. Nithad demanded that Volundr stay still, and not move any closer to the royal couple. He explained that the queen was distraught– the two young princes had been missing all day. No one had seen them since the evening before. The queen was in a heightened state of anxiety– bears had been spotted on the outskirts of the town that morning. Nithad had sent soldiers to search for the boys throughout the town and neighbouring forests. They had hunting dogs with them, hoping to catch the scent of the young princes. Nithad explained that the festival, and this evening's planned festivities had been suspended until he received news that the princes were safe.

"Volundr told the queen that he was sorry to hear this and assured her that news of her sons would surely come soon; it would be just a matter of time before she had them close to her once more. This seemed to appease the royal couple somewhat. Volundr continued: perhaps he could lift the queen's spirits, he added. He had brought gifts for the royal family with him. He told the king that their last encounter had not gone as he had hoped. He had worked hard for the kingdom since that time, crafting weapons and armour and fashioning jewellery. Volundr explained that he had prepared these special gifts so that Nithad might see how he had changed. He hoped that he could show himself to be a different man.

"Beside him, Bothvild grew excited. She knew that this was the moment when she would receive her new ring from Volundr, and he would ask her father for her hand in marriage.

"With Nithad's permission, Volundr reached into his bag and retrieved the gifts he had brought. To Sinmara and Bothvild he gave two jewel-encrusted ivory brooches. To Nithad he gifted two large silver goblets, finely crafted and similarly lined with delicate gems. Volundr added that it had been some time since he had last tasted the king's wine and hoped that they might do so together at tonight's banquet. He added that he been looking forward to tasting the traditional banquet meal: royal swan. Sadly, said Nithad, the swans had not yet returned this year.

"Finally, Volundr presented Bothvild with her new ring. He explained to the king and queen that this was to replace the old dull band that he said she had *lost*. This one was made just for the royal princess, he said, and more befitting who she was.

"The ring was exquisitely designed: the gold shank– coiled in parts and flattened in others– contained an inlay of solitary gemstones: a diamond to protect against illness, a sapphire to ward off evil, turquoise to heal and coral for fertility. Delicate diamonds similarly lined the gallery; a filigree design that curled its way towards the crown. Here, a large square ruby was set– the most regal of all stones– representing wealth, happiness and success in love. Surrounding the ruby was a rose pattern of gold, the petals formed from what appeared to be ivory.

"Bothvild was beside herself with happiness. The ring was everything she had hoped it would be. She slipped it onto her finger in an instant! She looked up at Volundr, overwhelmed by a feeling of deep adoration. Even in his current unruly state, she knew that she had never loved anyone as truly as she loved this man. Surely now was the time for him to speak to her father about *his* love for *her*.

"The conversation was cut short by the sudden and noisy entrance of the king's commander. Visibly distressed, he pronounced the kingdom to be under siege– from wild animals! The search parties that had been sent to the four corners of the town, armed with hunting dogs and items of the princes' clothing, had been met by bears and wolves and ravens. The beasts had been attracted to the same spots by some ill-chance and had proceeded to attack the soldiers and kill the dogs, before beginning a rampage on the outskirts of the town. Townsfolk were being terrorised, massacred— and it worsened by the minute as the beasts became overwhelmed with a lust for human blood!

"Nithad ordered the commander to leave at once: to gather *all remaining troops* at the four corners of the town: they were to push back the animals at all costs! Turning to the group, he explained that given the circumstances he had no choice but to cancel the mid-summer festival. It could not go ahead until the town was safe and the princes were found!

"Volundr looked at Nithad somewhat confused. What did he mean, 'until the princes were found'? Nithad grew angry and called the blacksmith a fool. Had he not been listening? The kingdom was under attack and the royal princes, the heirs to the throne, were missing!

"Volundr's demeanour had changed. The warmth in his face was gone. His brow was raised now, his eyes wide and wild, his lips twisted, his teeth bared. No— it was Nithad that was the fool, he said. For while they had all been in conversation, the princes had been returned to the castle. Could they not see?

"It was Nithad's turn to look confused now. A smile of disbelief flashed across his face. *How? When?* The queen sprung to her feet, demanding that Volundr explain what he meant by this.

"Volundr invited the royal family to look closer at their gifts, for the answers to their questions lay there. Volundr pointed to the queen, declaring that he had kept his promise: her sons were indeed close to her again. What were these fine, jewel-encrusted brooches, if not fashioned from the bones and teeth of her children? What did the silver on these two goblets

92

encase, if not the skulls of the young princes? What was the ivory on Bothvild's new ring, if not carved from the fine bones of greedy little hands? Volundr turned to Nithad now. Was it not time for them to share a drink and to celebrate the princes' return?

"Sinmara fell to the ground in utter despair. Nithad slipped backwards against the table, unable to summon the strength to call back his commander. Volundr continued: the town was indeed under siege by bears and wolves, mad for the scent of the boys' blood. He had led them towards town the night before, where they found it splattered across its walls. And yes— ravens too: plucking at the eyes of Nithad's soldiers and subjects. Volundr dragged himself over to the king, reached past him and retrieved a flagon of red wine from the table. He poured some into one of the silver goblets and raised it to the air in silent toast, drinking down its entire contents. Red wine splashed down his cheek, staining the front of his tunic.

"Bothvild was screaming now, the echoing sound filling the great hall. How could Volundr have done this to her? How could they ever be together now?

"Volundr looked at her, his face contorted with contempt. She should be happy now, he declared. She had everything she wanted. Bothvild had her parents' full attention, and with the princes gone she could be queen one day: the new heir to Nithad's throne. Though how she thought for one moment that *anyone* would want to share that throne with *her* was a mystery to him. Did she think he loved her? Did she think they were to be married? Volundr turned again to the fallen king. Stooping, he placed his hand on the shoulder of the man he despised more than any

94

other. He looked so small now, beaten. Volundr gestured towards the princess with his empty goblet. That's right: your daughter loved this wild beast. And in a calm voice, devoid of all emotion, Volundr spoke to Nithad:

"'Do not mourn the death of your sons. Cast your weeping eyes on the belly of your daughter. For therein lays the unborn child of your enemy!'

"Volundr straightened and reached into his bag to retrieve one final item. He shrugged his shoulders, nestling *Flygil* into position.

"A moment later …. he was gone."

9

"I need a cigarette," I said, rising from my chair.

I had remembered Wayland's story as soon as Borkham started to describe the princes. I had known what was coming, but at the same time I don't think I'd ever encountered it in so much detail, certainly not as a child.

Outside I took shelter, squeezing myself into the corner between the wall of the Inn and the outside wall of the porch. Facing the corner, I lit my cigarette quickly, shielding the lighter's flame from the blustering wind and the heavy rain. Turning around, I took a first drag, thrusting one hand deep into the pocket of my trousers. With the other, I hid the cigarette behind me, protecting it between me and the wall. Judging by the light, the sun was already starting to go down and the temperature was quickly following suit. Hints of the coming Winter were in the air. Once again I was regretting leaving my jacket in the car.

In the distance, through the heavy rain, the moor seemed to stretch on forever, cold and unsympathetic: from Fur Tor in the West– fog-enshrouded, sodden, remote – to Princetown in the South and HMP Dartmoor. You could see why they had built a prison there. It was hard to imagine anyone successfully escaping its high granite walls and fleeing across these moors, although many had. But this land could swallow a person at any moment, be it a prison escapee or a hapless walker: one wrong step could see you falling across uneven ground and into a half-lost tin mine or slipping into a peaty bog and sinking slowly to a bubbling death. Even in this modern age there were roads here rarely travelled, fields untrodden, marshland undisturbed. Out here the sound of a man in distress could be lost on the wind. Out here a body may never be found. How many dark secrets did this place keep? As I sheltered there from the rain and the wind, I could almost hear its answer:

There's always room for one more…

I lingered there a little longer, finishing my cigarette. I watched as the moorland mist rolled in from the tors: a silent accomplice to this murderous landscape. My boss– Nuth. That conversation before I'd headed up here. It hadn't gone well. It was never meant to go like that. But we'd done so much for him– helped him when he first arrived– And... I really didn't want to dwell on that right now. And it was so cold out here.

"'Fate goes ever as Fate must.'"

"I'm sorry...?" Back in the Inn, Borkham had been waiting for me, and wasted no time in continuing our conversation.

"It's from the poem. From *Beowulf*. I told you. Volundr is everywhere. Ev–"

"Everywhere is Volundr, yes." I was settling back into my chair, glad to be back by the fire. I placed my cigarettes and lighter in the space on the table where our emptied plates had been. "The rain hasn't eased up. And the mist is coming in now." The old man waved a hand as if to dismiss my small talk. For him, the weather was unimportant. There was a point to be made, and a captive audience with whom to make it. He leant towards me, and for a moment seemed lost in reflection.

"So strange to think how one moment might have changed the course of Volundr's life, might have sealed his fate. But when do you think it was? Was it that lake-side meeting with the maidens? Was it when he first drank the king's wine? The swans? Or was it as the lid of that chest slammed shut on the necks of the two young princes? Where was the crossroads where his life was forever changed? All these moments contained choices for Volundr, don't you think? Or do you think it was already written? Where did it go wrong? Or must Fate, as the poem says, 'truly go as Fate must?'"

"I don't know," I said, similarly caught up in the reflection. "It – it just seemed to spiral. Things got dark. Real dark, real quick…"

"'Round here we are superstitious people. It's all about the Devil and temptation, you know. You've heard the stories," he said. "Some will tell you that evil – it lurks on this moor. It skulks in the old mossy forests, it sleeps among the heathers and the gorse. They say it's like the land itself lays in waiting to lead you astray. Lead you astray to do the Devil's bidding... And stories about smiths? They are as old as fire, you know. They go back to ancient man– to when we first started dropping metals into the flames. For the first settlers here... they must've seemed like dark magicians, the men that could turn tin into bronze, make stronger weapons for the hunt. How easily they would have gained notoriety... No surprise that blacksmiths, the Devil... They're often seen as one and the same– connected at least..." He bent closer, whispering, as if to share a secret:

"Maybe it was like that for Volundr. Maybe in the mountains of Iceland, Volundr was visited by Him. Maybe in the remote Westfjords, something crawled up from the depths, from the ancient volcanic rocks... Disturbed by the digging for metals... Maybe somewhere there he made a pact, a deal– giving up his soul for a trade, a reputation. Perhaps he'd cursed himself from the beginning. That one moment? What if it was then, if it was *there?*" He tapped a finger slowly against the wooden surface of the table. "Maybe everything else was the aftermath of that pact... What do you think about *that?*"

"No," I said. "It's not that. Visited by the Devil? No– that's not Wayland's story. If there was magic in those mountains... I don't think it was that."

"It could've been. There are many versions of Volundr, like I said. Many *names*, many *stories*.

'Where now are the bones of that wise and famous goldsmith?'" he continued. He was savouring some poetic quote again, and behind his glasses his eyes had closed. And then– suddenly– they were open once more and staring at me. "It's a good question, don't you think? 'And who knows now *where* they may be?'" he went on. "What did happen to Volundr after that summer festival? Who knows indeed? Some say he *never died*... What if he cursed himself– was damned to walk the Earth for all eternity: some ghostly, heathen blacksmith, who's soul belonged in Hell...? Imagine that..." The question hung in the air between us; Borkham pausing, as if to heighten the drama of it.

"Hey–" The old man crooked his index fingers to his forehead and stuck out his tongue. His eyes glinted with glee: a devil face, a silly, almost childish pose these days. I smiled awkwardly.

After what seemed an eternity, he sat back in his chair, resting his hands in his lap.

I stared back at the fireplace. The fire had been restocked, re-stoked. I hadn't even noticed the landlord step past us to attend to it. No. Wayland hadn't seemed an evil man. Was there even such a thing? He'd seemed at times to be a kind-hearted soul, drawn to helping others: crafting for them, building for them. I couldn't see him as cursed and I couldn't see him as Devil-led...

"No – That's not it," I said. And then suddenly:

"Okay– maybe you're right," Borkham said. "That wasn't the moment– that isn't our story at all. I was just trying to get a reaction. You looked so serious when you came back in, is all. Besides, that would be the easy way out, wouldn't it? Blaming devilry." Borkham smiled at me. "Forgive me. No magic, black or otherwise...

And nothing up the sleeves neither," he said, holding his arms out in front of him. "Just a man I suppose," he said, looking at me across the table. "Just a man caught. A man caught up…"

I smiled back at him. I raised my hand, absently. I took a sip of ale and Borkham moved on:

"Okay then. So, tell me this… We've heard the details; we know what happened… So, how should we *feel?* Should we *sympathise* with Volundr? Should we *feel sorry for him?* Should we honour him in sonnets, *celebrate* his acts of violence on caskets? Is he a victim, or a vengeful assailant? Is he a hero, or is he a child murderer?" Borkham was leaning back in his chair now, arms folded. Moving from quote, to question, to quote… He was in his element, enjoying it. It was hard to know whether he was even looking for a response from me. I gave him one anyway.

"Like I said– what happened… It got really dark–"

"Of course it did! This story – I never said it would be a fairytale!" he said, pulling me back from my thoughts with a jolt. "What could have gone differently?" he continued.

"What do you mean?" The question caught me by surprise, almost as much as his sudden outburst.

"With Volundr! Taken from his home, his possessions stolen, trapped, crippled– enslaved! What if it were *you*? Or *me*? What would you have told *me* to do? What would you have *me* tell *you*?" Suddenly the old man had leant forward again and grabbed for my arm. He was looking into my eyes with an intensity that was unnerving. "What would you have *me* tell *you*?" he repeated. I wasn't sure what he wanted me to say. I felt uneasy.

"Wh– what happened next?" I asked, attempting to ignore the old man's hand, grasping at the sleeve of my shirt. He released his grip and pulled his arm back. A look of embarrassment fluttered over his face and through his beard I thought I saw his cheeks redden. He placed his other hand over the one that had been grabbing at me moments before, as if to hide it. He continued:

"What happened to Volundr next," he said, with a look of displeasure, "is the part of the tale that no one seems to care too much for. For many the tale is already told, the script written. The boys are dead. Volundr is free… But if you ask me," he said, "this is where the story begins."

"Go on," I said, curious where he would take us next.

"The truth is rarely black and white," he said, his composure returning now. He slipped back in his chair again, once more lost in thought. "Think about the events that had transpired after his maiming. It is easy to see that Volundr became–"

"The villain in his own story?" I asked.

"Exactly," he said. "You're getting it now." I wasn't convinced that I was. "So, let me ask you again. What would *you* do? What would you have told *me* to do?"

I pondered the old man's question. Could I live with myself after committing such crimes? I really didn't want to think about that. It was hard to see this simple smith as a predator, a child killer and a destroyer of kingdoms. And yet, there it was. Before I could answer, Borkham had moved on again.

"Let's take the story *this* way," he said, gesturing with his right hand, as if left or right had been two clear choices: two paths at an intersection. "Let's imagine *this* course of events. After the murder," he went on, "and the revelations at the great hall. After taking to the air and his escape– and let's be clear here, Volundr *did* get away, he did *get away with it*– he was carried by coastal currents, rising high above the ocean and to freedom...

"After some time in the air, he spied land and safety. He landed beside a river. It was quiet and still. He unfastened *Flygil* and began to wash away the events of the past few days: the blood, the dirt... Though try as he might, he could not remove the memory of it. Images flashed before him, replacing his own reflection: Bothvild, the princes, the horror of it all. In this peaceful spot, his mind could find no respite. He smashed his hands into the water— LEAVE ME ALONE!"

Borkham's voice had become too loud in that last moment, and I caught the eye of the two men standing at the bar. They had looked over, confused by the old man's words. A little concerned perhaps. I gave them a sheepish, almost apologetic smile. After a few moments, they looked away and returned to their own conversation. Borkham lowered his voice and continued.

"Eventually just a face stared back at him from the river. But whose was it? Whose was this brow, once softened with love and hope– twisted now with hatred and scorn? Whose were those eyes, once bright, now barren and lifeless? Surely this was not his own face in the reflection? A kingdom was torn apart, two boys dead and his own unborn child abandoned. Was he that lost to anger and vengeance and gore? Had he, as you say become the villain in his own tale? Volundr was forever changed... I imagine he felt great shame: so far from the man he once was, the husband he had vowed to be. I imagine him lost in the wilderness of his own mind, driven half mad with grief, anguish, guilt. A prison of the mind can be worse than any physical binding.

"And yet, somehow something of him survived. Weeks passed. Then months. The summer was replaced by falling leaves and the days grew slowly shorter. Over time a stillness returned to his soul, somewhere in the valleys and hills of this new land. If not peace, a passive... quietude was reached, between the songs of the birds and the breezes in the tall grass.

"Volundr made some kind of home for himself, an echo of the past. He hunted, he ate, he lived.... Eventually he rediscovered company and community. He met travellers, local villagers... He bartered and traded. A forge was built and once more he offered up his skills as a smith. He served this small community the only way he knew: shoeing horses, wheelwrighting… Again he fashioned simple rings… Slowly the one true Volundr returned and as the years passed, the sickening memories of that island began to fade, returning only in his most solitary moments. And in his dreams."

"So, 'Wayland the Smith lived out his days there, a happy man? *The End?*'" I shuffled uncomfortably in my chair. Like Borkham, I had been born not far from here. I'd been raised in Devon too. But *unlike* Borkham, I had travelled. I had *left* this rural life, seen a world outside. There were so many here, even in this modern age, that had never stepped outside their local area, let alone the county, the country. It was a quaint tale, and clearly the old man was fairly well-read. But the story had become a little trite now, a little naïve, and I was growing impatient.

"No, man– FAR FROM THAT!" Once again, the old man had become animated. I was shocked by the sudden change in his mood. He was surly now; frustrated, almost angered by my comment. I had been glib, it was true– flippant even. Surely Borkham's story deserved more than that.

"Volundr knew that he was living a lie! How could he *ever be happy*? He was deceiving these people. They saw him as just a friendly old blacksmith. He could never truly settle here. How could he, when deep within him there would always be this blight on his heart? Volundr was forever changed," he repeated.

"Finally, he told the local villagers one last lie: that wanderlust had returned. He said farewell to his make-shift home. He travelled again, as he had done in his youth. Although now the childish thoughts of an adventurous boy were gone, replaced instead by an iron-like resolve: Volundr would commit himself to penance. He would spend his days trying to right his wrongs, atoning for the bloody stains on his soul. He would travel far and wide, and whosoever needed his skills would find in him their just and humble servant."

I was staring into the fire again. It made sense to me. Like the heart of this fire, surely there was a spark, something in Wayland that could never be changed, never go out. Something that defined who he truly was, regardless of anything else, despite everything else. Part of his core, his soul if you like. Like the peat fire from the original Inn, you could move it from place to place, change the nature of the flame, but surely the same fire still burned… Borkham went on:

"He made his way across land and sea. He visited the Königreiches and the land of the Angles. He found himself in Gaul, Balcia,

Hibernia… Eventually his travels even returned him to his beloved Scandinavia…"

"Some of those place names… they're new to me," I said, amazed by what I was hearing. "And so, 'the legend of Wayland is born'…?"

"Not just 'Wayland'. OR Volundr," he said. "To some he was Welandu, Wiolant. To others he was Velentr, Velendes, Guielandus and Cuillean… Wilą-ndz and Walander… Galans… Truly he was a traveller of the world…"

The old man's eyes had glazed over, and he seemed to enjoy recalling all those names. I'll admit I was impressed. I had never heard most of them. Borkham had continued on, but I was lost in my thoughts. Vaguely, I could hear him musing 'Is there one true name, one true smith?' and tossing out statements like 'Not that old fool and his red hot tongs'. But I was taking in none of the detail. I was still struck by Borkham's list of names. How easily the old man had recounted them. I wasn't just impressed by his recall. It was by the pronunciation of the names too. It had seemed as though his Devonian lilt had dropped away for a moment; replaced by a specific accent for each name, spoken with diction and dialect. How many times had the old man sat in this chair, telling this story? Or maybe he had just been waiting to tell it, rehearsing in private, practicing over and over for a moment such as this. I hadn't expected this at all.

"And wherever he travelled, the stories *grew*," I said, my words drawing Borkham from reflection.

"Yes. And in all he became some form of craftsman," said the old man. "Devoted to creating, building, forging; serving... Volundr was *everywhere*– woven into their stories."

"They became the legends," I nodded. "That's how I'd heard of Wayland, and the Smithy in Oxfordshire–"

"Berkshire. Yes–"

"Sure, yes– the old stone barrow– that tomb. Legend has it," I said, recalling it now, "that if you leave a horse there and a suitable offering, when you return Wayland the Smith will have reshod the animal. And the money, the food– gone! There's an Inn there– like this one– close by– The... Horse... What is it– White Horse...? Yes! In the *White Horse Hills*!" Other Wayland tales were coming back to me now.

"It's at Olvricestone, yes– on the Ridgeway... There are stories of Volundr all along that old road. And these stories– yes– they *grew*, just as they had before his imprisonment. Although this time they included poetry and song. Volundr was worked into their legends, as you say; into their

117

fables, even their religions... He was celebrated, revered, heroised. And yet for him, nothing had changed. In his heart this he knew: despite his travels, his achievements, his years of devotion to selflessness and service... Despite it all... Volundr would never truly be free of that island. And the sins that could not be washed away...

"*This*," he gestured with his right hand, "is the road we took. And here is where the real story lives."

Borkham looked down, staring at the table between us, as if lost in thought. Moments passed. He picked up the short length of brown string once again, unravelling it. He pinched it between his work-worn fingers, rolling it now into a tight ball. "Everywhere," he said.

"Sorry?"

"Everywhere." He returned the ball of string to the table and looked up. He smiled at me, giving out a single, low laugh. "Hah! You want to talk about everywhere? Well, you don't need to look much further than *here*," he said.

"I don't understand," I said.

"This place, I mean," he said. "Where we are. The Pub. Did you see it when we came in? The old pub sign?"

"The Warren?" I asked. I wasn't following him. "The sign, out front? Do you mean the rabbits?" I remembered the sign from our arrival, fixed to the front of the Inn. The bricked-up window above the porch, the white words against the green board, the image itself at the top of the sign. But I wasn't sure what he meant or where he was going with his question.

"They're *hares*," said Borkham. "Not rabbits. They're three hares."

"Ah!– yes– of course!" I said. "The 'Tinners' Hares'. It's pretty popular around here. What about it?" It was true: the image of the three hares that chased each other in a circle was a common motif in these parts. How had I missed it? But I couldn't see why he was bringing this up.

"Oh, its popular alright," Borkham replied. It's in churches, cathedrals, synagogues… Pubs, houses… old places. Usually up high, on roofs. And it's not just the dozen or so that the old moorland miners put up neither. It doesn't get much more 'everywhere' than those old hares."

"How so?" I said.

"They're all over Europe. In the middle East too. China even. If you follow the right trails… They're the same everywhere. Different

120

countries, different religions but *the same thing*. Same design. It's uncanny."

"Yes, that happens," I said. "You do see that quite often: similar images, common motifs. But what has this got to do with—"

"Have a look at the ears. They're hares alright," he said. "But have a proper look. That's when you see. They only have three ears between them. Each hare only has one ear, but it's connected to the next ear on the next hare. Gives the impression that each one has two; that they're just three hares running around. But it's an illusion. They're joined up. They're forever connected, forever running around and around *together*, in an endless circle… A never-ending chase."

"I suppose they are," I said. It was frustrating. It was as if the old man was taking us down an entirely different path. One moment we were talking about Wayland the Smith and his travels, the next we were discussing the difference between a rabbit and a hare. I wasn't sure where this was leading. Perhaps it was time we brought the storytelling to a close.

"They *are*," insisted the old man. "It's intentional. And that's how you know it's the same old symbol... Not similar. *The same*... Uncanny," he repeated. "It's an old pagan symbol, you know? Around here, anyways. But it was the tin miners that put up these local ones. Much later," he said, gesturing around.

"Yes, that's how they got their name. When the buildings went up, so did the hares," I said.

"But why the hare? What's the significance of it? That's the million-dollar question, isn't it?" he said. "Wouldn't be your first-choice animal, would it, the hare?"

"I suppose not," I said. He was starting to appeal to my curiosity now. Where was he going with this?

"No– They get bad press these days, the hares, don't they?" he went on. "But the Saxons *loved them*. For them, the symbol of the hare meant lots of things: fertility, rebirth, eternal life even, and tied closely to their old Spring deity, Ēostre. Similar things elsewhere too, in the other countries, the other cultures… But here's the thing: as time moved on here, well – the hare's not exactly your cute little Easter bunny, is it? Not quite right at all. It didn't really fit with the plans of the day and the new religions. So, the old pagan hare– it got scrapped. Someone decided to change its path, give it a new destination. Just when it was getting comfortable.

"Suddenly everything's different: the *rabbit's* the new face of Spring. That old hare– it gets

123

demonised. One minute," he said, "you've got your own Goddess, and you're representing dawn, new life, and the coming of a healthy crop season... all the good stuff... the next– well– someone's rewritten your story. You're out of favour and tossed in with all the *evildoings*: you're a witch's disguise, you're the Devil's familiar. Suddenly," he said, pointing his finger across the table, "you're the villain."

"*The Witch Hare*– yes. I remember that story," I said. It was another of the old Dartmoor legends. A local witch that would turn into a hare to steal from the farmers.

"The rabbit's foot gets to be a symbol of good luck," he continued, tapping the table again with his finger. "But– Heaven help you if a hare crosses your path..."

"Yes... It's quite the fall from grace," I agreed.

"There you have it," said Borkham. "Meanwhile, you've still got this old symbol, the old *three hares* popping up on this building or that church, despite its reputation and all the bad press…" Borkham was shaking his head and scratching absently at his beard, as he mused over the idea. "How did some old cave drawing in Buddhist China make its way across the world though? Appearing on Persian textiles, ancient shields… on the walls and ceilings and stained-glass windows of holy buildings… only to pop up again later in gathering places like this one here, like this old pub? That's what no one can explain," he said.

"Maybe they just liked the image," I said. "They saw it somewhere else, as it drifted its way across the globe." I was growing tired of this train of thought now. It felt like a distraction.

"Who knows for sure? No one does... But it feels like something important," he said, deep in thought once again. "Like they were keeping it close, a reminder of the past. A connection to the old ways... It's on family crests... coats of arms... money... Just kept turnin' up–"

"Like the bad penny?" I said, smiling at the old man. I felt like we were a long way off from Wayland now and I wanted to get us back, to finish our story. "Hey– Maybe the sign on The Warren is part of some underground movement," I joked. I looked at the old man. "*Warren... Underground...*" I repeated. But Borkham was frowning now, still puzzling over his problem. "Or, what if the idea of 'rebirth' came to mean something else... Redemption? *Second chances?*" I was thinking about Wayland and trying to connect all this together. Trying to steer us back on track. And I was regretting my poorly timed joke.

"No. It was bigger than that," he stated, lowering his voice once again. "Those hares are there for another purpose entirely," he said.

"What sort of purpose?" I asked.

"What if they're there to serve as a *ward?*" he said.

"What do you mean?"

"Maybe the hares and their promise of Spring, their Goddess of life and hope... Maybe their images on the stone carvings, the wooden bosses, the plates, the copper coins... maybe they're *talismans*. There to protect. To protect the buildings or their owners, or whoever's in possession of the symbol... Maybe the people of the old religions knew the power of that symbol and it was there for that reason: to keep them safe on their travels."

"Like a St. Christopher pendant? Or the… is it the *pyanska*? Of Ukraine? Aren't they painted eggs?" I asked. I vaguely remembered seeing something like that on my travels through Europe.

"Yes. But it's more than that," said Borkham. The lines on his forehead had deepened as he ruminated on the idea. "And it was the same for our old miners," he said, leaning in towards me once again. "The Tinners' Hares were there to protect," he declared.

"What do you mean 'protect'?" I asked.

"To protect against evil, of course! Against the horrors… the horrors as old as time, that crawled up from the old dark mines. The night-things that emerged from the ground when evening came, and the mists rolled in from the tors. Maybe," he smiled, gesturing over his shoulder with a nod of his head, "in here *we're* protected from all that. Everything else must stay *outside*..." And in a hushed tone, almost a whisper: "Maybe that old pub sign keeps the Devil at bay."

There it was again: digging for metal and ancient evil. Borkham seemed to be revelling in it. Had he wanted his story of Wayland the Smith to disturb me, was that it? And when I hadn't been as affected as he'd hoped, had he contrived to spook me with something more sinister: a fireside tale, full of darkness and foul intent? Was that what all this had been about? The old man was grinning again now, grinning with that same childish glee as before. He had crossed his arms and was staring at me from the other side of the small table, waiting for my reaction. If this *had* been his intention, then it was he who was having the last laugh now.

"Maybe it's just a sign on a pub." I said, impatiently, a little uneasy. "Maybe it's whatever you want it to mean." I swept my right hand awkwardly out in front of me, gesturing across the table. The back of my hand brushed against the wooden surface and in turn seemed to sweep away Borkham's mischief.

"You're probably right there," he said, shuffling in his chair, lightening the mood. "I'm sure the hares wouldn't disagree. It's all in how your story gets told. The hares knew it," he said. "Maybe you're right! Maybe – all of it – it's just whatever you want it to mean. Even in *here*," he said, nodding his head, as if to gesture over his shoulder. "In this old pub… Maybe it's *all* just like the Tinners' Hares…"

An awkward silence fell between us for the first time. Borkham looked down at the table again. I felt embarrassed. Borkham had been sharing a side story with me – maybe having some fun at my expense – and my impatience, my clumsiness, had shut it all down. More time passed. Eventually, I said "And just like Wayland?" It was a gesture meant to encourage Borkham to take the reins again, as much as to pull us back to where we had been before.

"Oh! Exactly! Even for him… For Volundr," he said, becoming animated once more. "You're right, of course. With Volundr, men heard tell of his escape. How could they not? It followed him," he said. It was as if he was picking up where he had left off now, back on a familiar, well-travelled path. "It followed him, like a long shadow in the early morning sun.

"Men heard aspects of his tale and bent them to their will: his name came to stand for craftsmanship, confinement, cruelty; for valour, vengeance, invincibility... It is true that in the hands of some it was poetic..." The old man looked saddened for a moment, as if disappointed by the next detail. "But with others... they just revelled in the murder and the gore. It could never be avoided," he sighed, "and it would never be forgotten...

"Did you know," he said, "to this very day, in early December, the men of an island in Frisia, Germany... They dress in sheepskin and feathers to celebrate him? To celebrate 'The Flying Man'. They prowl the streets, 'hunting' for women. They terrorise locals... children... Eventually they 'flee to the sky', jumping off platforms and columns and into the waiting crowd. What do you think of *that*?"

"Never forgotten..." I shook my head as I repeated his words. In truth, I didn't really know how to respond.

"Oh yes," he said, his voice suddenly becoming brighter. "But on the other hand, there are those who don't remember Volundr at all. Don't know his story, have never heard of him... Perhaps *that* is for the best— Perhaps..." He sighed, pausing for a moment. "Perhaps his tale should be allowed to run its course. Perhaps it is time we allowed his hearth to burn down to clinker... Maybe for Volundr *true peace* can only be found in anonymity... As the poem says: 'That was overcome, so may this be.' After all," he mused, "there is not much use for a blacksmith anymore."

"True...True... Borkham, I must ask you, coul–"

I never finished my question. At that moment we were startled by the sound of a hunting horn. I whipped my head around towards the bar– the direction of the sound– just in time to see the two men bursting into laughter, the landlord attempting to wrestle a large brass horn from one of them and struggling to return it to a shelf behind the bar.

I looked back at Borkham. He looked as surprised as me. "It's getting late," he said. I agreed. The tale– we had been so lost in amongst it all, unaware of how much time had passed. But now it was told. Here we were. And my bladder was full.

10

I rose from the table and stepped away from the fire, making my way through the bar. I wasn't getting it– Borkham's story. Wayland's fate was to travel the Earth, trying in vain to make amends for past wrongs. Point taken. The old man had been hung up on Fate and Free Will, choice and chance. Granted, the story had taken a gory turn, but it was nothing I hadn't heard before. What was I meant to take away from this? What was he trying to tell me, if anything?

Nuth knew all about Free Will, all about choice and chance. He just took whatever he wanted.

Sarah didn't understand. She expected me to be more like him. But I had been busting a gut, giving EVERYTHING for the firm – ME! And there *he* was, just taking all the credit, taking whatever he wanted. I had tried to explain that to him. It hadn't gone well. There was going to be questions asked. I should not have gone to his house. And I shouldn't have been driving so fast on the moor. All of this could have been avoided. I should be done with this damned place by now! There was so much still to do.

I washed my hands. I looked in the mirror. I looked tired, stressed. It barely even looked like me, truth be known. I really needed to get away. I ran my wet fingers through my hair. I straightened my tie. In the bar the clock struck seven. Outside, it would be dark.

When I returned to the bar the old man was gone. I walked to the small square table by the fire. There were the two empty chairs. There was my packet of Dunhills and my lighter. The pint glasses, drained of their contents, were gone. In the centre of the table: a short length of brown string, neatly rolled into a ball. I picked it up, smiling to myself. "Well, it looks like he left as suddenly as he arrived," I said, to no one in particular. My mind wandered to the recovery vehicle. It surely couldn't be too far away now, anyway. *Swing by, pick me up, head back to the intersection at The Watching Place.* Such a straight stretch of road outside The Warren. I wondered whether I might see its headlights coming in the distance. I grabbed my belongings from the table, returning them to the breast pocket of my shirt. I headed to the door. One last cigarette while I waited.

The rain had stopped, and the wind had dropped away. The lights outside the Inn created pools of orange and white that pushed back at the darkness and the inevitable moorland fog. I put the cigarette to my lips. I never got to light it. In one such pool sat a Nissan Qashqai, shining and stark white against the backdrop of the moor. It looked almost new.

I could barely believe my eyes. I walked over to my car in disbelief; a feeling that never left me, as I realised immediately that the car was no longer sitting with a slight lean– as if the corner was sinking slowly into a Dartmoor bog. On a closer inspection, my suspicions were confirmed: the driver's side tyre was no longer flat but looked as new as the day it had left the factory floor.

On the bonnet of the car was an old grey nail. I picked it up carefully and moved it around in my fingers. It looked almost hand-made: stunted with square edges. I had seen one of these somewhere before, but I couldn't quite place it. I put the nail into the pocket of my trousers. I started to walk back towards the Inn door. What had happened? What did I miss while I was away from the bar? Had the recovery vehicle arrived at the crossroads and replaced the tyre, before bringing the car here? Why hadn't they stopped here to pick me up first? Had they come into the Inn to look for me? Where was the driver now? Surely there would be some company paperwork to complete. Surely they wouldn't just leave me the offending nail and be on their way. All these questions rushed through my mind. And *where was Borkham*? Where was the old man? I couldn't see his van. Why had he left so suddenly? And what about my car ke–

Suddenly I was overwhelmed by a feeling of panic. I rushed back to the car.

WAS EVERYTHING THERE? WAS EVERYTHING HOW I'D LEFT IT?

I opened the driver's door – there in the centre console were the car keys. In the glove box: my phone. I'd turned it off hours ago. But what about the rest? I reached over to the back of the car. There, on the back seat was my jacket, where I'd thrown it to make room for Borkham. I grabbed it and wrestled myself into it. It felt good to finally have it on after all this time. Under the jacket had been my laptop, the light on the side blinking silently, reminding me that I had unfinished work. I walked around to the rear of the car and opened the boot. There inside was Nuth, just as I'd left him.

He was lying on his right side, his mouth closed over with silver duct tape, his hands behind him, bound by the power cord of my laptop. His legs were bent, with tape wound tightly across the cuffs of his business trousers. In the struggle to bind his legs, the trousers had slid up a little, exposing his socks, an inch or so of skin and some leg hairs. This added an awkward, almost comical element to his appearance, and for a moment I was reminded of bicycle clips, and men who cycled to work. For the first time I noticed that one of Nuth's loafers was missing– it was who-knows-where. Both feet rested against the spade that was wedged up against his knees, ready for when it would be needed. Nuth was not wearing his jacket, and one side of his business shirt had come untucked. I could see now that the wound on his head had stopped bleeding. The blood that caked his forehead had dried and was beginning to flake. It glittered as it caught the light from the Inn...

All of these details I took in, as if seeing Nuth for the first time. I hadn't wanted to think about him being there, or about what would be happening next. Out here the sound of a man in distress could be lost on the wind. Out here a body may never be found.

Nuth was awake now. The anger and contempt in his eyes had been replaced by mute pleading. I found myself thinking about the intersection and The Watching Place, thinking about an old man and his tale of escape. I think he'd told me that I too was escaping from something. Was it the rain? Was it the flat tyre? *Was it getting away with this?*

I was still holding the cigarettes and lighter. I shoved them down into the pocket of my jacket. The penknife was still in there. I fumbled with it— distracted, allowing it to roll around in my hand… Opening it slightly with my thumb, I played with it: now open, now closed, now open, now closed… In my mind I saw an old blacksmith, smiling as he huddled over his work. Two young boys are sitting beside him. They smile back at him as he sharpens a blade. I thought about Wayland– a man forever changed.

"So, does *Fate go ever as Fate must...*?" I said, to no one in particular.

I remembered the nail then. I pulled my hand from my jacket and pushed it back into my trouser pocket. I pulled out an old grey nail, stunted with square edges. It was a horseshoe nail– too blunt surely to pierce a car tyre.

(You'd thrown a shoe!)

I'm thinking about a small blue van at a crossroads, its hazard lights blinking in the rain. The inverted image of a signpost in the rear-view mirror. In my mind I'm seeing a pony in the road. It's staring straight ahead... I'm seeing my car skidding, lurching as I drag the wheel to the right... Tyres are screeching ... And there's Beetor Cross– The Watcher... Ancient oaks, an old mossy forest... gnarled and twisted limbs that are reaching for me, daring me to come closer.... There's a face at the passenger window of the car...

I'm looking down at Nuth, shivering in the boot of my Nissan Qashqai. Only 500 miles on the clock. He's looking almost child-like, folded up that way. I'm struggling to remember how it had all come to this. It just seemed to spiral. Things got dark. Real dark, real quick. I'm looking down at Nuth. I'm thinking that it had something to do with Sarah... Sarah and Nuth... I'm still holding the nail. I'm seeing a pair of weathered hands, poised on the lid of an oak chest. I'm imagining the drive North, and the detour to Fur Tor– fog-enshrouded, sodden, remote. I'm thinking about putting my hands on the lip of the boot, closing in Nuth and getting into the car.

I'm thinking about an old man in an Inn. An old man and his tale of escape. Yes— yes *he had*; he'd told me that I too was escaping from something. Was it the rain? Was it this moor— this damned moor? Or was it— what had he said?— 'a fate worse than death'…? I can almost see him, the old man: an open hearth spitting and popping. He's sharing a tale as old as fire. *A cautionary tale?* And I think there are hands— hands again? Are they reaching across a table? Are they grasping at my shirt? And what is it— what is it he's saying? I can't be certain anymore. It's distant now, hazy for me. It's my head. I'm not sure of anything. But… no— it's not a haze… it's a mist. It's like a moorland mist, rolling in from the tors. Rolling in, closing me in. A mist that's in my head.

Volundr. I think I'm seeing Volundr now. He's stepping from a line of trees; shielding his eyes from the sun as he looks across the clearing to sounds coming from a lake. I'm looking down at Nuth. I'm thinking about the intersection at The Watching Place. I'm thinking about whether I should slam the boot shut.

Acknowledgements

A special thankyou to my wife, Kylie for her support and encouragement. Thanks for making room for me to do this mad and solitary thing called writing.

To *Daidállō*'s other early readers: Amy, Ang, Donna, Garry, Louise, Rachel, Richard, Sarah and Ursula… Thanks for humouring me when you didn't know what you were getting yourself into. Thanks for taking the time to read this story and for your kind words.

To Anthony, Donna, Jim, Kerry, Matt, Nik and Tia… Thank you for your support. To

Acknowledgements

Russell – a special thanks for all your enthusiasm. It means the world to me.

To Eddie: As I wrote this story, I was glad to be reminded of work we had done together, many moons ago, particularly the collaborative piece we did for *20 Years of Heavy Metal*– a Hell-ride across Dartmoor in a beat-up borrowed Morris Monor. It seems that *The Devil's Footprints* led to Brisbane too. You are always generous with the opportunities that success affords you. Not enough ales and tales pass between us these days, but I raise my glass to you in eternal gratitude, my friend. Perhaps, somewhere in a corner of Warren House Inn, the ghosts of two other residents linger, hunched over spectral beers and snickering like schoolboys concocting another prank. The next round is on me.

To Nathan, my oldest and dearest friend: the River Taw may spring on Dartmoor, but it is at its strongest as it flows through the town where you and I have walked and talked many, many times. My head and heart (and notebooks!) are fuller for our friendship. You have always been so selfless with your time and spirit, and for *Daidállō* it was no different. We will both be forever grateful. Proper job, my 'andsome.

To my daughter, Adeline, my partner in crime: you never get tired of hearing the crazy nonsense that's rattling around in Dad's head. Thanks for amazing me every day. Never stop being you, sausage.

To Lewis: thank you for kicking this off with your excitement and wonder. I hope you enjoyed Wayland's story, my son.

Finally, to you, dear reader. Thanks for picking this book up and for making it this far. My hope

Acknowledgements

is that *Daidállō* left you intrigued, curious, entertained.

I hope that you're glad that you got into that van with us and that we all sheltered a while from the storm.

Marcus Moore

Launceston (the other one)

April 21st, 2025

About the author

Marcus Moore is an English born writer and publisher who now lives in Tasmania, Australia with his wife and two children.

He co-founded, edited, and contributed to the anthology books *Different Voices* and *DeeVee*.

Photo by Adeline Moore.
Taken at Two Bridges, Launceston.

As well as being an author of longer fiction, Marcus has written for publishers in the graphic medium, including Penguin Books, Kitchen Sink Press, Dark Horse and Heavy Metal, and has ghost-written for a popular syndicated cartoon strip.

www.ingramcontent.com/pod-product-compliance
Lightning Source LLC
Chambersburg PA
CBHW051512260626
47162CB00008B/2939